OCTONAUTS™

and the Giant Squid

OCTONAUTS WHO'S WHO

The daring crew of the Octopod are ready to embark on an exciting new mission!

INKLING OCTOPUS
(Professor)

KWAZII CAT
(Lieutenant)

PESO PENGUIN
(Medic)

BARNACLES BEAR
(Captain)

TWEAK BUNNY
(Engineer)

SHELLINGTON SEA OTTER
(Field Researcher)

DASHI DOG
(Photographer)

TUNIP THE VEGIMAL
(Ship's Cook)

EXPLORE . RESCUE . PROTECT

OCTONAUTS™

and the Giant Squid

SIMON AND SCHUSTER

Professor Inkling was busy baking fish biscuits, when Dashi's face flashed up on the videophone.

"We've just received a call from Captain Barnacles!" she cried.

The Professor rushed out of the galley.

"I'll be right there!"

The big screen on the control deck showed Captain Barnacles and Kwazii exploring some amazing underwater caves. Professor Inkling settled down to watch, when the GUP-A suddenly began to s-h-u-d-d-e-r and shake.

"We're under attack!" radioed the Captain. "Barnacles out!"

Something **enormous** was gripping the back of the sub!
It took all of Barnacles' polar bear strength to wrestle
the GUP-A's controls.

"Arrgh!" cried Kwazii. "I can't see what's got us!"
The Octonauts held on tight as the mystery monster
turned the GUP-A upside down.

"We're getting out of here!" decided the Captain, pushing the engine up to full speed.

The GUP-A's paddles flapped frantically. But just as the sub broke free, the monster squirted it with a strange, black fog.

"Shiver me whiskers!" yowled Kwazii. He couldn't see a thing!

When the fog cleared, Barnacles flicked on the videolink.

"Octonauts, we're OK," he told the crew. "Prepare to open the Octohatch!"

Kwazii and Barnacles docked in the Launch Bay, then
Tweak checked over the GUP-A.
  "It's covered in slimy ink, Cap'," she puzzled.
"And what are these marks?"

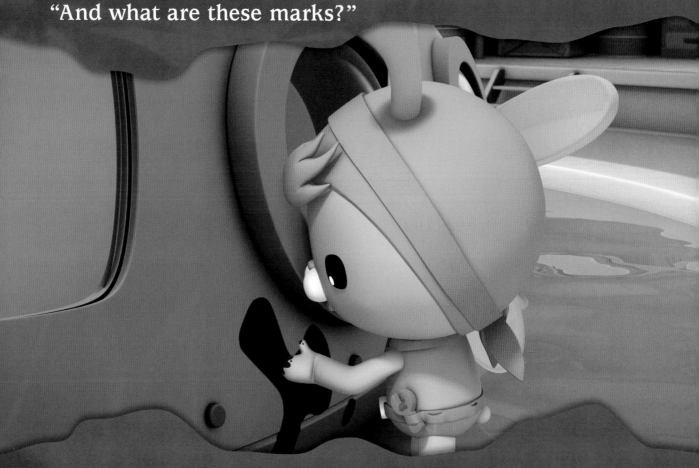

Professor Inkling studied the strange sucker prints covering
the back of the sub.
  "Unless I'm very much mistaken," he announced,
  "they were made by my cousin Irving, the giant squid!"

Dashi pressed some buttons and a picture of Inkling and his cousin appeared on the Octopod computer.

"This is the only picture I've got of Irving," sighed Inkling.

Kwazii looked confused. "Why would your cousin use his suckers to grab the GUP-A?"

"I think he was scared," replied Inkling. "We need to make sure he's all right!"

Barnacles nodded. "Professor, sound the Octoalert!"

"Octonauts, to

"Octonauts, our mission is to find Inkling's cousin, the giant squid!" announced Barnacles. "Kwazii, Peso, into the GUP-A."

"I don't usually come on missions, but Irving is family," said Professor Inkling. "If he needs help, then I should be there too!" The Captain agreed. **"Let's do this!"**

The Professor jumped aboard. Before the sub could set off, Tunip handed up a basket of fish biscuits.

"Thank you, Vegimals," smiled Inkling.

But Tunip wasn't finished. He passed up another basket and then another and another until…

"Woah!" waved Barnacles. "That's all the biscuits we have room for!"

It was time to open the Octohatch!

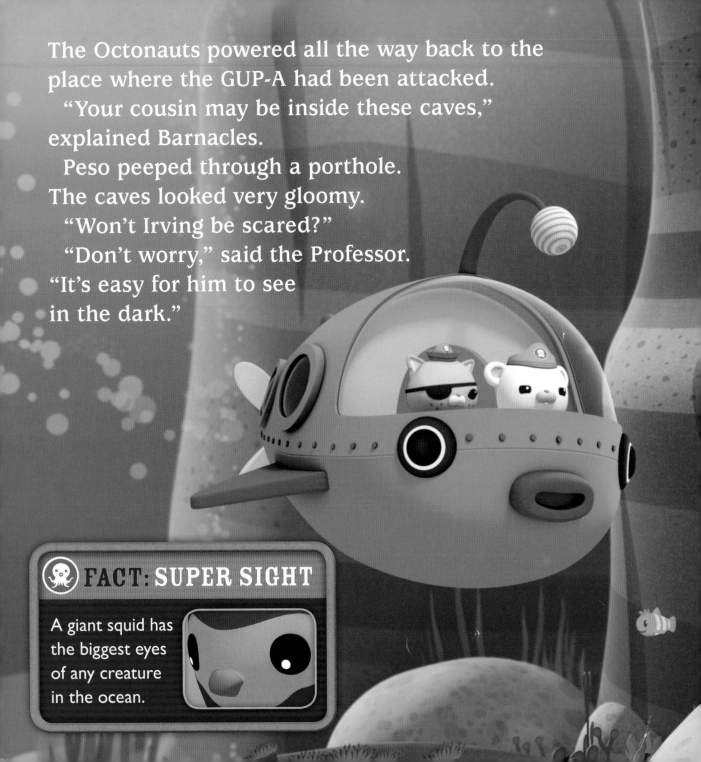

The Octonauts powered all the way back to the place where the GUP-A had been attacked.

"Your cousin may be inside these caves," explained Barnacles.

Peso peeped through a porthole. The caves looked very gloomy.

"Won't Irving be scared?"

"Don't worry," said the Professor. "It's easy for him to see in the dark."

FACT: SUPER SIGHT

A giant squid has the biggest eyes of any creature in the ocean.

Barnacles, Peso and Kwazii swam out to search the caves, while the Professor stayed behind to keep a look-out.

Tracking down Irving wasn't going to be easy. Peso was sure he'd spotted the squid, but it just turned out to be a row of rocks.

Next Kwazii shouted out, but all he'd found was a manta ray.

Even Barnacles' special creature detector only managed to locate an eel!

Back on board the GUP-A, Professor Inkling was finding it tricky to resist the delicious fish biscuits. "What a wonderful smell!" he sniffed. "Perhaps a little snack will cheer me up while I wait."

Suddenly a pair of giant red tentacles gripped the GUP-A. "It's... it's cousin Irving!" yelped the Professor.

Barnacles, Kwazii and Peso splashed back to find out what all the commotion was about.

"Inkling!" shouted the Captain.

The GUP-A was in the grips of the biggest giant squid the crew had ever seen!

There was no need to worry. Irving didn't mean any harm to the Octonauts – he was just feeling peckish!

"I've been looking for food all day," explained the hungry squid.

"So that's why you grabbed the GUP-A," guessed the Professor. "You thought it might be food."

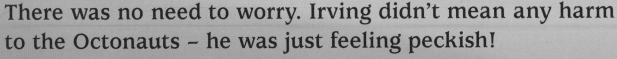

Inkling paddled straight out with a basket of biscuits.

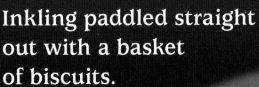

"So how did you find each other?" asked Barnacles.

"I smelled those fish biscuits!" grinned Irving.

"A giant squid has an excellent sense of smell," explained Inkling. "Here, have another basketful!"

As soon as Irving's tummy had stopped rumbling, the Octonauts took him back to meet the rest of the crew.

"This is the Octopod," beamed Professor Inkling. "My home away from home!"

Irving was very impressed.

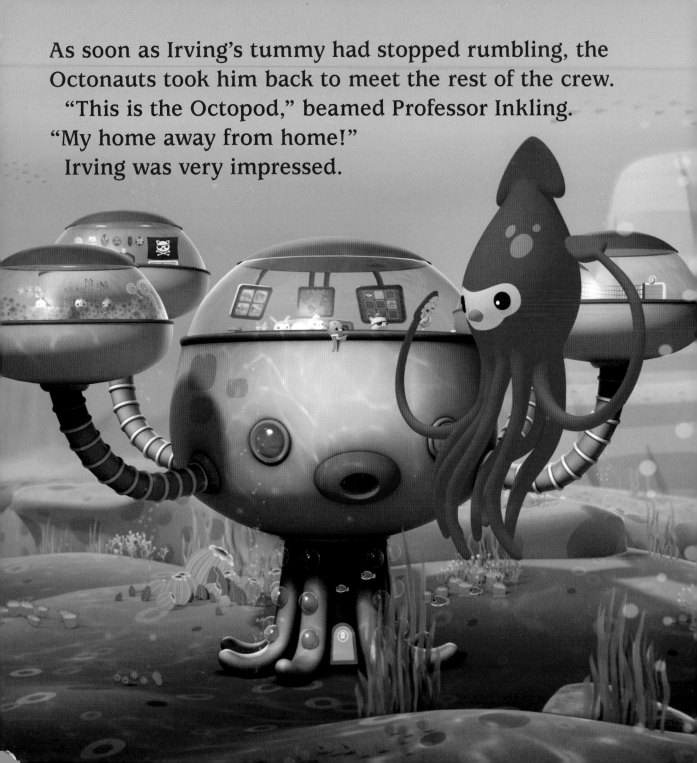

Dashi bobbed up with her underwater camera.
It was time to get a new photo for
the Professor's family album.
  "Move in closer please,"
she called. "Perfect!
Now say seaweed!"
  The cousins waved,
showing their best smiles.
  "Seaweed!"
  A happy snap of Irving
and the Octonauts –
Inkling would treasure
it forever!

☻ CAPTAIN'S LOG:

Calling all Octonauts! After the GUP-A narrowly escaped a squid attack, our hunt for Irving began! We discovered that Professor Inkling's cousin has big eyes, enormous tentacles and a giant appetite to match.

FACT FILE: THE GIANT SQUID

The giant squid is a colossal sea creature. Its arms have suckers, just like an octopus!

 It lives in the Twilight Zone.

It eats fish and squid.

OCTOFACTS:

1. The giant squid has the largest eyes of any creature in the sea.

2. It squirts ink when it's scared, so it can run away without being seen.

3. The squid has an awesome sense of smell.

OCTONAUTS™

Dive into action with these super, splashtastic Octonauts books!

OCTONAUTS
As Seen on TV!
Ready for Action in the GUP – A!

OCTONAUTS
As Seen on TV!
and the Electric Torpedo Rays

OCTONAUTS
Meet the Crew
As Seen on TV!
Press the button and sound the OCTOALERT

OCTONAUTS
As Seen on TV!
and the Decorator Crab

OCTONAUTS
As Seen on TV!
and the Giant Squid

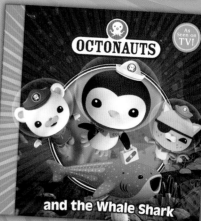

OCTONAUTS
As Seen on TV!
and the Whale Shark

WWW.THEOCTONAUTS.COM

www.simonandschuster.co.uk